Mr. Ape

DICK KING-SMITH

Mr. Ape

ILLUSTRATED BY ROGER ROTH

SCHOLASTIC INC.

New York Toronto London Auckland Sydney
Mexico City New Delhi Hong Kong

ISBN 0-590-81925-9

Text copyright © 1998 by Fox Busters, Ltd.
Illustrations copyright © 1998 by Roger Roth.
All rights reserved.
Published by Scholastic Inc., 555 Broadway, New York, NY 10012,
by arrangement with Crown Publishers, Inc.
SCHOLASTIC and associated logos are trademarks and/or registered
trademarks of Scholastic Inc.

12 11 10 9 8 7 6 5 4 3 2 1   9/9 0 1 2 3 4/0

Printed in the U.S.A.   40

First Scholastic printing, January 1999

CONTENTS

Mr. Ape

I

Ape Has a Brainstorm

FOR SOME TIME NOW, Archibald Peregrine Edmund Spring-Russell of Penny Royal had slept in his kitchen.

It was not on account of a shortage of bedrooms. In fact, there were fifteen bedrooms in Penny Royal, a huge, rambling barracks of a house given to an earlier Spring-Russell by King Charles II for services rendered.

The reason was a simple one. The kitchen was enormous, the kitchen was warm, and the kitchen was where Archibald cooked, ate, and spent most of his indoor time. So he thought, Why not sleep there? And he moved his bed down.

Archibald Spring-Russell lived alone at Penny Royal, and the few people who came to the house—the mailman, the milkman, the coalman, the man who came to read the meter—addressed him as Mr. Spring-Russell. Not that he ever said much to any of them—he was a man of few words. Some people thought him grumpy, but in fact his manner was really due to shyness. Had any of his old friends (of whom he hadn't many) come to visit (which they didn't), they would not have used the name Archibald, nor Archie, nor any of his other names. They would have called him by the nickname he had acquired as a schoolboy, when, because of his initials, he had been known as Ape.

Strangely, this name fit him. He had been a large, shambling, loose-limbed boy, and now he was a large, shambling, loose-limbed old man, who walked around with his long arms hanging low, as though at any moment he might drop onto to all fours.

Ape lived alone at Penny Royal for the simple reason that his family had left him. His children (in whom he had never been very interested) had grown up and gone out into the world, and when the last one left, his wife had said, "Right, Ape, I'm sick of this big ugly house and I'm tired of you, so I'm off."

For most people this would have been upsetting after thirty years of marriage. But though at first surprised by it, Ape found that he was really rather relieved.

At last he had the place to himself (for his wife before leaving had dismissed all the servants), and he thought, I can do as I like. For Mrs. Spring-Russell was a very bossy lady, and over the last thirty years Ape had done as he was told.

One of the things he had been told was that no animal of any kind might be kept at Penny Royal. His wife had considered them dirty, and his children had never been the least bit interested in pet keeping.

Whereas Ape as a boy had kept chickens and rabbits and guinea pigs, and had lavished on them rather more affection than he had later been able to feel for his sons and daughters, with whom he had little in common.

For one thing, they didn't have much of a sense of humor.

Once he had said to them, "Do you know what you are?"

"No," they said. "What?"

"You," said Ape, "are the Offspring-Russells." But they all looked at him blankly.

Nor were they particularly nice. They were, in fact, quite horrid, selfish and uncaring and rude to the servants.

For the first week or so after the departure of his wife and all the servants, Ape made a vague effort to keep the enormous house clean and tidy, but this, he soon realized, was too much for an old man to do, even an old man who was still strong. So he decided to shut up most of the place.

First he shut up fourteen of the fifteen bedrooms. Then he closed the doors of the huge high-ceilinged living room and the long lofty dining room and the music room and the sewing room and the flower room and the library and the billiard room and the butler's pantry.

Then Ape shut up each of the dozens of other rooms in Penny Royal, except for one bathroom and the kitchen. A couple of weeks later, finding that he spent a good deal of his time in this last-named room, he was able to shut the door of the fifteenth bedroom after spending a day moving his four-poster bed to the kitchen. He dismantled it, maneuvered it bit by bit down the great curving central staircase of the house, and reassembled it nice and near the warmth of the big old-fashioned coal-fired range on which food for the Spring-Russell family had been prepared (and later, after they had finished their meals, food had been prepared for the cook and the butler and the parlor-maid and the two housemaids and the boy who cleaned the boots).

After a while, Ape found that he rather enjoyed cooking for himself. Always before, his wife, in consultation with the cook, had chosen the menus for the day. But now Ape could make all his favorite meals, things he had liked as a boy. Sausages, for example, and grilled-cheese sandwiches, and fish sticks, and rice pudding that he mixed with crumbled-up graham crackers and strawberry jam. And eggs—boiled, fried, poached, scrambled—Ape was particularly fond of eggs.

Doing the shopping all by himself was another new experience that was fun, so much so that every day he drove into town in his ancient but well-preserved Rolls-Royce and spent a lot of time in the super-market choosing schoolboy food.

Before long it occurred to him—as he was putting a carton of eggs into his shopping cart—that here was something he needn't buy. He could keep his own hens to provide his own eggs at home, at Penny Royal!

He thought excitedly about his idea that evening as he sat up eating his supper of turkey burgers and curly fries and baked beans, with ice cream to follow. Now that he had things properly arranged, Ape only ate lunch at the big wooden kitchen table. His breakfast and his supper he ate in bed.

"I shall buy some hens," he said (to himself but out loud—it was nice to be able to say things without fear of contradiction from his wife). "But where shall I keep them?"

Because of Mrs. Spring-Russell's aversion to animals, there was no such thing as a chicken coop at Penny Royal. There were stables (where no horse had been allowed) and kennels (where no dog had set foot), and even a large stone dovecote (from which no dove had ever flown).

"It would be possible," said Ape, "to keep hens in one or another of those. But they would not be very comfortable in such cold, drafty places, and then if I let them out in the daytime, there's always the risk of a passing fox. What they will need is somewhere

warm and dry and comfortable and safe and roomy. But where?"

When Ape had finished his ice cream (cookies and cream), he got out of bed and put his dirty dishes into a bowl in the kitchen sink to soak. Then he put on his bedroom slippers and an old bathrobe and went out of the kitchen and along a passageway that led to the great central hall of Penny Royal.

Down this hall he shambled, long arms hanging, deep in thought, passing the closed doors of the various rooms. He stopped by chance outside the living room. Absently he opened the door, walked in, and looked around at the deep armchairs and sofas, at the heavy pieces of furniture, at the rich, soft carpets.

On one wall of this large room was a full-length portrait of his wife, dressed in a ball gown in a hideous shade of blue, looking her bossiest. Ape stood before it, staring up.

"I," he said, "am going to keep some hens, and you can't stop me! But where shall I keep them?" he asked as he turned away.

Then it was that A. P. E. Spring-Russell, Esquire, of Penny Royal in the county of Gloucestershire raised one of his long arms and smacked himself on the forehead with a shout of joy.

"Right here!" he cried. "It's warm and it's dry and it's comfortable and it's safe and it's roomy. I'll keep my hens in my living room!"

2

Ape Goes to the Market

THE FIRST THING TO be done, Ape realized, was to get rid of the deep armchairs and sofas, the heavy pieces of furniture, and the rich, soft carpets, none of which would be of any use to hens. Nor would the grand piano, nor the occasional tables with their ornaments, nor the long velvet curtains, nor the gilt-framed paintings on the walls.

"I shall sell them all," Ape said to his wife's portrait, "except you. You can jolly well stay up there and keep an eye on my hens. Come to think of it," he went on, "I might as well sell every stick of furniture in the place that I can part with. Actually, I've got almost everything I need in the kitchen."

So before long a great sale was held at

Penny Royal, to which buyers came from all over the country. They saw no sign of the owner, Mr. Spring-Russell, though some of them noticed two things. First, the kitchen door bore a large sign that read:

PRIVATE. KEEP OUT.

And second, in the living room there hung a portrait of Mrs. Spring-Russell with a small sign that read:

NOT FOR SALE.

"Tragic!" they said to one another. "The old chap's shut himself away—can't bear to see his precious belongings sold. But he won't part with the picture of his beloved wife."

Once all the furniture had gone, Ape came out of hiding and walked all over the house, visiting each room and enjoying its bareness. Last of all he came to the living room, empty of everything but the portrait and beneath it Mrs. Spring-Russell's favorite armchair, a large high-backed ornate thing that looked like a throne.

Ape had instructed the auctioneers to put a NOT FOR SALE sign on it as well. He had always hated the chair, and hoped that his hens would dislike it too and sit on it and show their feelings in the proper manner. He stamped happily around it, his steps loud on the large expanse of bare floorboards.

"Now," he said, "I can buy my hens. But first I must provide for them."

So he made several trips into town in the old Rolls-Royce, loading it with sacks of chicken feed and a metal bin to store it in, and feeding troughs and water troughs and many bags of sawdust.

It was not until the living room was ready to receive its new occupants—the feeding troughs and water troughs filled and the sawdust spread over the floorboards— that Ape realized what was missing. Perches!

The birds would need somewhere to perch at night.

Later Ape sat up in bed eating hamburgers with ketchup and worrying about the problem, for the next day—market day—he planned to buy his hens.

Suddenly he saw the answer right in front of his eyes.

Suspended from the high ceiling of the kitchen, and lowered by a system of ropes and pulleys, were several long wooden racks used in the past by the staff of Penny Royal for drying all the laundry in the house. The racks were in effect aerial clotheshorses, but it took no time at all for Ape to convert them into down-to-earth hen perches.

He lowered them, cut through their supporting ropes, carried them off, and set them up in the living room, then went happily back to bed, finished his supper, and went to sleep.

Ape woke the next morning with that thrilling feeling of something very exciting about to happen. He boiled eggs for his breakfast—the last eggs he would have to buy—then got back into bed and sat up, dipping thinly sliced pieces of toast into them.

"What sort of hens will they have for sale, I wonder?" he said. "And how many shall I get? I can buy as many as I like—the living room's plenty big enough. I wonder what color they will be. I hope they'll lay brown eggs—I like brown eggs."

And then, as he swallowed his last piece of toast, another worrying thought suddenly occurred to him.

"Nest boxes! They must have somewhere to lay those eggs, instead of just dropping them anywhere on the floor."

As he dressed in the clothes he always wore—a hairy tweed suit of an old-fashioned cut and brown boots—he stood in the middle of the kitchen settling the knot of his old school tie and worrying about this problem of nest boxes.

Then once again he saw the solution right in front of him. Against the wall stood a tall old kitchen cabinet of pale-colored wood. Beneath its high shelves were six drawers—drawers that were filled with an army of knives, forks, and spoons.

"All I need is one of each," said Ape, and he collected up the rest of the silver-ware and dumped it into a cupboard.

Then he took out the six drawers and laid them along one wall of the living room, three on each side of Mrs. Spring-Russell's chair (which was just beneath her portrait).

Now all was ready.

Ape put on the old brown curly-brimmed bowler hat that he always wore to go to town and drove off in his Rolls-Royce.

No sooner had he shambled into the covered part of the market that housed the poultry for sale than he saw exactly what he wanted.

There, in a wire cage, were twelve big beautiful brown hens. Many other pens had birds for sale—white ones, black ones, spotted ones—but Ape hardly gave them a second glance.

By the time the auctioneer came to sell the hens, Ape, having found an ice cream truck, was licking away at a large ice cream cone (his second) of his favorite flavor, strawberry.

When the bidding began for the dozen brown hens, other farmers and poultry keepers made their bids by a nod or a wink or a tap on the nose or a pull at an earlobe.

Ape bid by holding his strawberry ice cream cone aloft. And hold it up he did, time and again, until the price rose so high that all the others dropped out, and the birds were knocked down to him.

"Sold to the gentleman in the, er, brown hat," said the auctioneer. "Your name, sir?"

"Spring-Russell," said Ape.

"Address?"

"Penny Royal."

A moment later one of the haulers approached Ape, offering to deliver the hens. "I'm going your way, sir," he said.

"Don't need you," said Ape, "but I'd be obliged if you'd crate them up and stick them in my car...."

"You never saw anything like it," the hauler said later to a group of his friends in the pub. "There's this big old guy dressed like I don't know what, and he pays the earth for a dozen hens and gets me to put 'em along with a bale of straw in a couple of crates and stow 'em on the backseat of his car, which just happens to be a Rolls-Royce Silver Ghost, and you'll never guess what he gives me for a tip."

"Ten pence?" they said.

"A ten-pound note," said the hauler. "They don't breed 'em like that anymore. Ten quid, just for lifting a couple of crates. You could have knocked me over with a feather."

You wouldn't even have needed a

feather to knock the hauler over if he had seen, sometime later, twelve big beautiful brown hens wandering contentedly around the vast living room at Penny Royal, pecking in the feeding troughs, sipping from the water troughs, fluttering up to try out the perches.

To put the seal on Ape's pleasure, one of them almost immediately hopped onto the chair and proceeded to lay a beautiful big brown egg right under Mrs. Spring-Russell's nose.

3

Ape Has Visitors

EARLY THE NEXT MORNING that first egg was followed by several more. Soon after waking up in his four-poster bed in the kitchen, Ape heard the triumphant cackling that every hen makes after laying coming from the living room, and knew he now had two eggs for his breakfast.

Later, sitting up in bed eating them, he heard more cackles, and by the time he was dressed and had returned to the living room, a half-dozen more eggs lay in the drawer nest boxes.

In fact, despite making himself scrambled eggs for lunch and an omelet for his supper, a couple of eggs were still left over by the end of the day.

"Well done, girls!" Ape said proudly

when he went to say good night to his big beautiful brown hens. "I can see I shall have quite a time keeping up with you."

The last of the daylight coming in through the tall French windows showed them dozing on their clothes-rack perches, muttering sleepily to one another.

The next day Ape happened to look out the French windows. Where he normally would have expected to see a great sweep of beautifully mown lawns, he saw instead what looked like a hayfield. So busy had Ape been within the walls of Penny Royal that he had given no thought to what was happening outside.

"Blimey!" said Ape. "Of course! She must have sacked the gardeners as well."

The grounds of Penny Royal were extensive and had needed the attention of two gardeners and a garden boy. But now, as Ape found when he went out to walk around, the place was like a jungle.

Apart from the overgrown lawns, the

flower beds were choked with weeds, as was the kitchen garden, where many of the vegetables had gone to seed. Everything was in a terrible mess.

Stopping first outside the French windows of the living room to admire his hens within, Ape went back indoors and made himself a large cup of cocoa. He sat dunking cookies in it.

Over the years he had made a secret study of the art of dunking—secret because Mrs. Spring-Russell strongly objected to the practice. He knew the exact length of time a particular variety of cookie could be immersed before becoming too soggy and therefore disintegrating into the cup. Graham crackers were a two-second dunk, ginger snaps three, shortbread cookies four, chocolate chip five, and so on.

As he ate his shortbread cookies (four seconds), Ape discussed with himself the problem of the overgrown grounds.

"I can't possibly manage it all," he said.

"That's for sure. All that mowing, weeding, sowing, hoeing, that sort of stuff. I suppose I'll have to get the gardeners back. If they haven't found other jobs.

"On the other hand," he continued, "I don't really want to do that. Does it matter if it's all a bit jungly? There's no one else to see it but me. Though I must say it looks a frightful mess."

When he finished his cocoa, he went out into the kitchen garden and pulled some lettuce for his hens. Fetching a stepladder and some string, he suspended the greenstuff from the giant glass chandelier that hung from the center of the living room ceiling.

While he was watching the birds pecking happily away at the lettuce, Ape suddenly became aware that someone was watching him. He turned toward the French windows and saw the mournful face of a donkey staring in at him. Ape noticed that around its neck was an old rope with a frayed end to it. It was plain to see that the creature had been tethered to a post or peg, and the worn rope had snapped, setting it free.

At that moment Ape heard a loud knocking, and he made his way out of the living room, shutting the door carefully behind him, and crossed the hall to the enormous double front doors of Penny Royal.

"Must be the mailman," he said (for the milkman and the coalman and the man who came to read the meter always used the tradesmen's entrance). But when he opened the doors, he saw, standing at the top of the broad flight of stone steps that led up from the forecourt, a boy wearing rather ragged clothes and a worried look.

"'Scuse me, mister," said the boy. "You haven't seen a donkey, have you?"

"Yes," said Ape. "On my lawn on the other side of the house."

The worried look vanished from the boy's face and was replaced by a broad grin.

"Oh, thanks, mister!" he cried. "She's my

donkey, you see. Dada bought her specially for me. She's named Columbine, and she broke her tether. Our caravan is parked on that big piece of common land up on the hill, and we searched all over it but couldn't find her, so I came here."

"Where's your father, then?" asked Ape.

"He's looking in the fields on either side of your drive," said the boy. "I'll call him." And he put a finger in each side of his mouth and let out the loudest, most piercing whistle imaginable.

"Gosh!" said Ape admiringly. "I've always wanted to be able to do that."

"I'll teach you," said the boy.

"Thanks," said Ape. "What's your name, by the way?"

"Jake."

"Come on, then, Jake. Let's go and catch your Columbine," said Ape, and he shambled down the steps, the boy following.

As they set off, Jake pointed down the drive.

"Here's Dada coming now," he said.

Ape saw a tall man, with longish black hair like the boy's, striding toward him. He looked angry.

"Hey, you," he said loudly. "Where d'you think you're taking my boy?"

Ape looked the tall man in the eye (they were about the same height).

"I'm taking your boy to show him where his donkey is," he said, "and I'll tell you something: he's a good deal more polite than his father." And he turned his back on the man and walked on. Jake and his father followed.

But when they reached the lawn-turned-hayfield, there was no sign of the donkey.

"Funny," said Ape. "She was standing just out here." And he pointed to the French windows, behind which stood several of his hens looking out from the living room, while others continued to pull at the lettuce hanging from the chandelier. From the wall behind, Mrs. Spring-Russell seemed positively to glower at the sight of Jake and his father looking in.

They found Columbine in the overgrown kitchen garden, eating a very large cabbage. The man took hold of her rope, while the boy scrambled up onto the donkey's gray back. He leaned forward, pulling gently at her long ears and crooning some sort of song to her in a language Ape could not understand.

"Thank you, mister, thank you very much," Jake said, smiling at Ape. Ape smiled back. This boy, unlike Ape's wife and children, obviously loved animals.

"Sorry," said Jake's father abruptly. "I shouldn't have spoken to you like that, sir. I was worried. I didn't know where Jake had got to." He put out a hand.

Ape shook it. "Forget it," he said. "What's your name?"

"Hart. Joe Hart."

"You're Gypsies, aren't you?"

"We call ourselves Romany."

"You're in a caravan, up on the common, Jake was telling me," Ape said. "I've always fancied life in a caravan, moving around the countryside wherever you like, here today, gone tomorrow, always the open road stretching away before you."

"I daresay you're more comfortable in a great house like this," said Joe Hart.

"I'm as snug as a bug in a rug," said Ape. "It's the outside that's worrying me, this kitchen garden, the lawns, and all the rest of it. It's one big mess."

There was a short silence, broken only by the noise of the donkey chomping cabbage. A look passed between father and son, and then Joe said, "I could lend a hand for a bit if you like, sir."

It's a good strong hand, too, thought Ape, and the boy could be useful if I should get some more livestock, which I might. Anyway, he's going to teach me to whistle with two fingers.

"All right," he said. "Thanks. We'll try it. I'll pay you a fair hourly rate, and you can bring Columbine with you, and she can eat her way through this jungle. Does she pull the caravan?"

"Oh, no, sir," said Joe. "I've got a horse."

"A pinto, he is," said Jake, "named Billy."

"Well, bring him too," said Ape, "and look here, Joe, there's no need to call me sir. My name's Spring-Russell, but I've always been known by my initials, you see. A.P.E. Call me Ape."

"Couldn't do that," said Joe. "Wouldn't seem right."

"But we could call him Mr. Ape, couldn't we, Dada?" said Jake.

"No, no," said Joe.

"Yes, yes," said Ape.

4

Ape Gets Some Pets

A WEEK LATER THE view from the French windows of the living room was rather different.

His hens clucking contentedly around him, Ape looked out once again at the broad lawns of Penny Royal.

Joe had spent hours mowing them, and had at last made them look much more respectable. Each day he and Jake had brought Columbine the donkey and Billy the horse and turned them loose in the walled kitchen garden, where they feasted.

"Good thing you can't see them in there," Ape said to his wife's portrait. "You'd have forty fits."

Jake came into the living room.

"Mr. Ape?" he said.

"Yes?"

"Do you like rabbits?"

"To eat, d'you mean?"

"No, to keep as pets."

"Haven't kept any since I was your age."

"You could now," said Jake. "In the dining room. They'd have lots of space to run about."

Before Ape could comment on this, they heard a noise somewhere up inside the living room chimney. It was a scrabbling noise, like something falling. First down came a shower of soot with some bits of stick mixed in it, and then into the wide, empty grate fell a bird.

"What on earth...?" began Ape.

"It's a jackdaw, Mr. Ape," said Jake. "A young jackdaw. There must be a nest of them in the chimney top, and this one's come tumbling all the way down."

"Catch him," said Ape, but before the boy could lay hands on the bird, it began to flutter around the floor, much to the surprise and annoyance of Ape's hens, who ganged up and began to attack this soot-blackened intruder.

The fledgling jackdaw had not yet mastered the art of flying, and things would have gone badly for it if Jake had not grabbed it. It squawked and pecked at him, but he talked to it and soothed it, and soon it stopped struggling, regarding them both with bright black eyes.

"What shall I do with him, Mr. Ape?" Jake asked.

"Well," said Ape, "we can't put him back up the chimney, and we can't let him loose in the world since he can't fly well enough yet. So we'll have to keep him, Jake, if he is a he, which we don't know. He can live in the kitchen with me."

"He'll make messes everywhere, Mr. Ape," said Jake. "But you could keep him in the dining room. The rabbits wouldn't mind."

"Rabbits?" said Ape. "Oh, yes, rabbits, I remember. You were saying? Tell you what, Jake. We'd better go shopping."

· ▰ ·

The following morning Ape made himself one of his favorite breakfasts, a breakfast quite unlike most people's.

First he opened a can of creamed rice, poured it into a bowl, added two big spoonfuls of strawberry jam, crumbled some graham crackers into the mixture, and stirred it all up together with a spoon.

Next he hard-boiled three brown eggs from his brown hens, squished them up with a fork, added salt, pepper, and a large lump of butter, and stirred that up.

Then he got back into bed and sat up against his pillows, happily eating these strange mixtures and chewing over the idea of buying himself some rabbits. He clearly remembered a particular pet rabbit he had had as a small boy seventy years ago, and how fond of it he had been. He could picture it still, looking out through the wire of its little hutch.

Ape swallowed his last mouthful.

"I suppose," he said as he got out of bed to put the dishes into the sink, "that that rabbit would have been happier if he'd had room to stretch his legs. Not much space in a hutch. Still, there'll be messes in the dining room. Also, I'd better get several rabbits—for company, you know."

Ape continued talking to himself as he dressed. "I'll drive into town today," he said, "and have a look round the pet shop and see what they've got. Perhaps Jake would like to come with me. I'll ask Joe if he can."

He found Joe in the stable yard, cleaning the Rolls-Royce.

"Where's Jake?" he asked.

"Looking after Columbine, I expect," said Joe. "He fusses about her like nobody's business."

"Why?" said Ape. "She's not ill, is she?"

"No," said Joe. "She's in foal. Six months along, so only another three to go."

"Wow!" said Ape. "Going to have a baby, eh? How wonderful! I'd love to see a baby donkey born here at Penny Royal. I do hope you won't have gone before then—I know Gypsies are always moving. How long do you plan to stay on the common?"

Just as Ape finished speaking, Jake joined them. "We won't leave for a while, I hope, Mr. Ape," said Joe. "Jake here has enrolled at the village school, and the term starts soon."

"I suppose you've had to go to quite a few different schools, eh?" Ape said to the boy.

Jake nodded. "I wish I could stay at the same one, like other children," he said. "But as soon as I've made some friends, we move on again."

"The trouble," said Joe, "is the same it's always been. People don't feel comfortable with Romany folk. To them we're foreigners at best, who sell clothespins and sprigs of lucky heather, eating hedgehogs baked in a clay oven. At worst, they think of us as a pack of dirty thieves and try their best to get us moved somewhere else. We ought to be all right where we are now—it is common land—land where we are free to stay, but sooner or later someone will find a way to get rid of us. It isn't so much that we want to keep moving on—it's that we have to."

"Couldn't you buy a piece of land?" said Ape. "No one could put you off it then."

"Land costs money," said Joe. "Which I haven't got."

I have, thought Ape. More than I know what to do with.

Joe gave the windshield of the Rolls a final going-over and stood back to admire his handiwork.

"She hasn't been so clean for donkey's years," said Ape. "Which reminds me, I'm going into town this morning. I'm thinking of buying some rabbits."

"Rabbits?" said Joe. "To eat, you mean?"

"No, I don't want to eat them," said Ape. He laughed. "Though I am going to keep them in the dining room," he added. "Now, would it be all right if Jake came with me? He might like a ride in the Rolls, and I'm sure he'd be a help to me in choosing these rabbits. He's good with animals."

"That's fine by me, Mr. Ape," said Joe. "I know you'll take good care of him."

• ♠ •

The road to town crossed the common, and as they drove over it, the Harts' caravan came into sight, a big old-fashioned horse-drawn caravan, brightly painted in red and blue. Ape slowed and stopped.

"Jake," he said, "d'you think I could have a peek inside your home? It looks so nice."

"'Course you can, Mr. Ape," said Jake, and they got out of the Rolls and walked across the grass toward the caravan.

"Aren't you afraid someone might steal

from it?" Ape asked. "Now that you and your father are down at Penny Royal all day?"

"No," said Jake. "Swift wouldn't let them."

"Who's Swift?" Ape asked.

As an answer, Jake put a finger in each corner of his mouth, and out came that piercing whistle. Out, too, from under the steps that led up to the back door of the caravan came a thin, long-legged, snake-headed, tawny-colored dog with dark spots, a lurcher that ran to Jake and licked his hand, whip tail wagging.

"She's going to have puppies, Mr. Ape," Jake said.

"Wow!" said Ape. "Your donkey's in foal and your dog's in whelp. Aren't you lucky!"

Inside the caravan Ape immediately noted how neat and colorful it was, with bright paint and burnished brasswork and lots of gleaming ornaments. There wasn't a speck of dust to be seen. This was the home of a very house-proud person—though "caravan-proud" would perhaps be better.

Jake pointed to a large color photograph in a gilded frame that hung upon the wall. It was of a raven-haired woman—not much more than a girl, Ape thought—who stared unsmilingly at the camera. Her face, with its high cheekbones and large dark eyes, was beautiful.

"That's my mama," Jake said. "She died."

Ape nodded. Joe had told him that his wife had died when Jake was small, and that he was bringing up his son alone.

"Your father told me," he said.

He thought of adding, "How very sad" or "I'm so sorry" or "You must miss her," but something inside made him say no more. Poor little chap, he thought.

Jake seemed to know what Ape was thinking. "It's all right," he said, as though Ape was the one who needed comforting. "She died when I was very young. I can't really remember her."

When they arrived in town, Ape and Jake went first to the bank, where Ape withdrew some money, and then on to the pet shop. They were a strange pair, Ape in his hairy tweed suit, brown boots, and brown bowler hat, Jake in old jeans and a T-shirt and sneakers, the tall old man lumbering along in his usual way, the boy positively skipping in his excitement.

"How many rabbits are you going to buy, Mr. Ape?" he asked as they walked along the main street.

"Depends on what they've got," said Ape.

In fact, the pet shop had four rabbits for sale—a black one, a gray one, a spotted one, and a white one with pink eyes.

"What d'you think, Jake?" said Ape.

"They're all really nice, aren't they?"

"Well, we'll take all of them, then."

"But, Mr. Ape," said Jake, "hadn't you better ask whether they're bucks or does? Bucks might fight when they're put together."

"You're right," said Ape, and he asked the shopkeeper.

"The white one's a buck," the man said. "The other three are females."

"Well," said Ape again, "we'll take all of them, then."

"But, Mr. Ape," said Jake again, "you'll have to keep the buck separate or else you'll have dozens of rabbits before long."

"Good," said Ape.

His eye fell on two large cages full of guinea pigs. "Look at those, Jake," he said. "I used to keep some when I was your age. I like guinea pigs. They make nice noises, talking to you all the time." And to the shopkeeper he said, "All right to keep rabbits and guinea pigs together, is it?"

"If you've got plenty of space."

"I have," said Ape.

"How many did you want?"

"How many have you got?"

The shopkeeper counted the guinea pigs. They were of many different colors, some with smooth coats, some with rough, some long-haired. "There are twelve here altogether to choose from," he said. "Was it boars or sows you wanted?"

"Don't care," Ape said.

"How many would you like?" asked the man, and, for the third time, Ape said, "We'll take all of them, then."

"But, Mr. Ape," said Jake for the third time, while the man was putting the animals into boxes, "you haven't asked him how much the rabbits and the guinea pigs are. Surely you want to know?"

"I don't care," said Ape.

"How will you manage, sir?" the man asked, looking at the sixteen cardboard carrying boxes.

"We'll stick 'em in the car," said Ape. "Be back shortly." And in five minutes the owner of the pet shop, for the first and only time in his life, found himself loading four rabbits and twelve guinea pigs into a Rolls-Royce Silver Ghost.

Back home at Penny Royal, Joe helped to carry the boxes in. On Ape's instructions he had already spread a thick layer of sawdust all over the dining room floor and put food ready, and now the three of them watched as the rabbits hopped silently and the guinea pigs ran squeaking around the place. Despite Columbine's best efforts, the kitchen garden still had tons of vegetables, and soon the new arrivals settled down to feast on a heap of cabbage and carrots. The jackdaw was already much stronger and greeted them with loud squawks.

"Nice, aren't they, Joe, don't you think?" said Ape.

Joe shook his head, smiling.

"Hens in your living room, now rabbits and guinea pigs and a jackdaw in your dining room! Whatever next, Mr. Ape?"

"To tell you the truth, Joe," said Ape, "I'm thinking about using the music room next. It would be the proper place, it seems to me."

"The music room? What for?" Jake asked.

"You heard them in the pet shop, didn't you, Jake?" said Ape. "Singing beautifully, they were. I've always fancied keeping some canaries."

5

Ape Has a Birthday

APE AND JOE AND Jake stood in the music room looking around. It was a small room by the standards of Penny Royal, at one corner of the house. It had two large windows, one at each side of the right angle, and it was very light.

"Why's it called the music room, Mr. Ape?" Jake asked. "Was there a piano in here?"

"No," said Ape. "The piano was in the living room."

"Oh," said Jake. "Well, if they made music in the living room, what did they do in the music room—live?"

Ape laughed. "Actually," he said, "my wife fancied herself a harpist. She used to play her harp in here."

"Like the angels do in Heaven?"

"Don't know about that," said Ape. "I thought she made a devilish noise. Canaries will sound much sweeter."

Joe looked around the bare room. "They'll need somewhere to perch, Mr. Ape," he said.

"So they will. Pity that old harp's gone. We could have rigged it up on its side, and then they could have perched on the strings."

"Begging your pardon, Mr. Ape," said Joe, "but that would never have done. My father always had a canary in his caravan, and I remember him telling me about perches. People give canaries perches that are much too narrow, he said, no thicker than a pencil, and that leads to cramping and sore feet and sometimes even broken joints. A canary's perch, he said, must never be less than half an inch wide."

"Let's go up into the attic," Ape said, "and see what we can find. When I sold most of the contents of the house, I never bothered with all the junk that's up there."

In the attic Jake's sharp eyes caught sight of something in among the rolls of old carpet and odds and ends of furniture. It was a bag of golf clubs, and stenciled on the pocket were the initials A.P.E.S–R. A narrow, old-fashioned bag it was, and in it was a set of nine wooden-shafted clubs.

"These would do for perches, wouldn't they, Mr. Ape?" Jake said.

"Golly whiskers!" cried Ape. "My first clubs, the ones I had when I was a boy!"

He pulled them out one by one.

"Driver, brassie, baffy, mid-iron, mashie, mashie-niblick, jigger, niblick, and putter," he said, using the old names by which they had been known in his young days.

He gauged the width of a shaft between his finger and thumb. "Half an inch!" he said.

So it was that by the time Ape and Jake returned that afternoon from a second expedition to the pet shop, Joe had the music room ready.

He had fixed several lengths of strong twine across the room from one molding to the opposite one. From these each of the golf clubs was suspended by a long string fastened to either end of it, like a trapeze. Each club had been hung at a slightly different height, and each made a perfect perch for the three pairs of canaries that Ape had bought.

Ferreting around in the attic, Joe had found a box full of old kitchen junk and had taken from it saucers and bowls for seed and water. He had also filled an empty cookie tin to act as a bath.

"I remember," he said, "that Father's canaries used to love to have a bath."

Around and around the music room the six birds flew, chirping to one another with joy at this newfound freedom, and before long one pair actually settled on a golf club (the putter, it was).

They perched there side by side, their little feet gripping the hickory shaft comfortably. Their combined weight, tiny though it was, was just enough to set the trapeze swinging gently.

"Perfect!" said Ape. "Great idea of yours, Jake. And Joe, you've fixed it all up beautifully. Fancy those old clubs coming in so useful. I was given them for my twelfth birthday, I remember."

"When is your birthday, Mr. Ape?" asked Jake.

"August twenty-sixth."

"That's tomorrow!" said Joe.

"Is it?" said Ape. "Is it really? Well, well! I tend to forget about birthdays at my time of life. My family never seemed to remember mine anyway. But I'll tell you what. This year I feel like celebrating it. Come to tea, both of you."

"You come to us, Mr. Ape," said Joe. "Come and have your birthday party in the caravan."

"Oh, yes, thanks. What fun!" said Ape. "But only if you'll let me bring all the grub."

· ▲ ·

Early the next morning Ape went to the door in his bathrobe and slippers to answer the mailman's knock.

"Morning, Mr. Spring-Russell," the mailman said. "And a beautiful morning it is, too."

"It is, by Jove!" said Ape.

He did not say it was his birthday, though later he did examine the mail more carefully than usual. But no one had sent him so much as a card. However, it seemed to him that his canaries were singing even more tunefully than ever in the music room, that in the dining room his rabbits were hopping more happily, his guinea pigs chattering more cheerfully, and the jackdaw squawking more raucously. And what's more, as though to celebrate the occasion, every single one of his twelve hens in the living room had already laid him a beautiful brown birthday egg.

After scrambling some for his breakfast in bed, he dressed in his usual clothes and drove into town in the Rolls to buy what he needed for the party.

"There ought to be a birthday cake, I suppose," he said as he drove along (never exceeding thirty miles per hour—he did not approve of speeding). "But I won't bother with candles. I'd need too many. And I'll jolly well have my favorite sort— a great big chocolate seven-layer cake, full of frosting."

In the supermarket Ape filled his shopping cart with exactly the things that small children like best (because they happened to be the things he liked best, too).

To drink he bought soda and lemonade, and to eat he bought cream-filled cupcakes, powdered doughnuts, chocolate chip cookies, brownies, and, of course, the cake.

At teatime Ape drove the Rolls up to the common, and they all carried the food into the caravan, sat down, and had a feast.

When at last Ape could eat no more, he sat back and patted his tummy. "That was good!" he said.

Suddenly he heard little squeaking noises coming from the basket in which Swift was lying. He looked at Joe and Jake, his eyebrows raised questioningly.

"Yes," said Joe. "She whelped this morning."

"Look, Mr. Ape," said Jake, and there beside Swift were four tiny puppies. Ape gave a low whistle.

"Golly whiskers, they're adorable!" he said.

He saw Joe look at Jake and nod, and then Jake said, "We've got a present for you, Mr. Ape, but you can't have it yet."

"Oh, my!" said Ape. "I didn't expect a present."

"You'll have to wait a couple of months," said Joe.

Ape frowned, puzzled.

"It has to stay with its mother for now," said Jake.

It suddenly clicked. Ape's frown turned into a huge grin, and he pointed at the basket in the corner of the caravan. "D'you mean . . . ?" he began.

"We'd like you to have the pick of the litter, Mr. Ape," said Joe.

6

Ape Gets Nice Surprises

THAT NIGHT APE FOUND it hard to get to sleep in the big four-poster bed in the kitchen. He was too excited.

When he was young, he had never had a dog of his own, and once Mrs. Spring-Russell came onto the scene, there was no chance of his having one. Now—or at any rate in a couple of months—he would be the proud owner of the pick of Swift's litter!

"I wonder which one I'll choose," he said. "And what shall I call it? Depends on whether I get a male or a female, I suppose. Which shall I get? By Jove, what fun it all is!"

When at last he stopped talking to himself, his last thought before he fell asleep was that of all his seventy-five birthdays, this one had been the nicest.

Ten days or so later, something happened that took his mind off the puppies.

It was Jake who noticed it first. Because he was so good with the animals, Ape was happy to have Jake help with the care of the hens, the rabbits, the guinea pigs, and the canaries.

One morning a few days before he was due to start at the village school, Jake came out of the dining room and ran across the hall and down the passageway to the kitchen. "Mr. Ape! Mr. Ape!" he called excitedly. "The spotted one's plucking!"

Ape turned around from the sink, where he was washing up the breakfast dishes (he'd had fish sticks and baked beans and sour-cream-and-onion potato chips, a mixture of which he was very fond).

"Plucking?" he said. "Spotted one? What on earth are you talking about, Jake?"

"The rabbit!" Jake said. "The spotted doe. She's plucking the fur from under her chin and off her chest to make a nest. She's going to have babies soon."

"Golly whiskers!" said Ape. "She would be, wouldn't she? The rabbits must have been here nearly a month now."

"You'll have to move her, Mr. Ape," said Jake, "and the other two does as well. They can't stay in there with the buck and all the guinea pigs and the jackdaw, and anyway there's nowhere for them to make their nests. They can't just have their babies in the middle of the dining room floor. Where can we put them?"

Ape thought.

"Got it!" he said. "In the butler's pantry. That's the place! Not too big, nice and snug, and there's a row of cupboards at floor level all along one wall—where the silver was kept. Open the doors of those, and they can each choose one."

"They'll need some stuff to make their nests with," said Jake. "As well as their own fur, I mean. Some nice soft hay."

"Of course, of course," said Ape. "Come on, let's move them straightaway."

So they did.

In the butler's pantry the three does—the spotted, the gray, and the black—hopped curiously about, noses working, and before long the spotted doe picked up a mouthful of hay and carried it into one of the open cupboards.

"We shall have lots of rabbits soon, won't we, Mr. Ape?" said Jake.

"Yes," said Ape, "and lots of guinea pigs, too. I suppose we'd better start thinking about them."

"No hurry," said Jake. "Rabbits take thirty-one days to have babies, but I expect you remember that guinea pigs take more like seventy. Because their babies are born with their fur on and their eyes open and they start eating almost immediately. We needn't worry about the guinea pigs yet."

"Of course," said Ape. "I remember now. Gosh, Jake, I don't know what I'd do without you."

A couple of days later the rabbit population of Penny Royal tripled when the spotted doe gave birth to eight babies in the butler's pantry. By then both the black and the gray doe had each chosen a cupboard and were plucking.

All this excitement had kept Ape from going to see the puppies, and then, just when he had determined he would go up to the common the very next day, something else happened.

It had become the custom for Joe and Jake, at the end of each working day, to come into the kitchen for tea and cookies.

"Well, Jake," said Ape as he dunked a cookie (chocolate chip—five seconds), "it's a special day for you tomorrow, eh? Starting school, aren't you?"

Jake nodded.

"It might be a special day for someone else, too, Mr. Ape," said Joe.

"Who?"

"Columbine. Looks like she might foal tonight. If it's all right by you, I'll bring her into the stable, and Jake and I will stay with her. She might need help."

"Of course, of course," said Ape. "I'll come down later to see how it's going."

When Ape entered the stable, he found that Joe had bedded Columbine down in a stall.

"Anything happening?" he asked.

"She'll be a while yet, Mr. Ape," said Joe.

"I'll wait up with you."

"No need. I'll come and tell you when she foals."

"No, no, I wouldn't miss this for the world," said Ape. "Tell you what, I'll go and make us a Thermos of cocoa and some sandwiches. Spam all right?"

The cocoa drunk, the sandwiches eaten, the three of them sat side by side on a bale of straw, their backs against the wall, waiting and watching.

Try as he might, Jake could not keep his eyes open. He fell asleep leaning against his father. The hours passed, and the old man, like the boy, could not stay awake, and his chin dropped onto his chest. When he woke again, it was to see Joe and Jake kneeling beside something that lay in the bedding of the box, something small and blackish and wet that was making little snorting, gasping noises as its mother licked it.

As Ape levered himself to his feet, Joe looked up, smiling.

"A filly foal!" he said.

Awkwardly, for his old joints were stiff, Ape lowered himself onto his knees beside the newborn child. "Shall you keep her, Joe?" he asked softly.

"No, Mr. Ape. When she's old enough, I shall sell her."

"To me?"

"If you like."

7

Ape Makes a Deal

NOT UNTIL THE DONKEY foal had managed—after several unsuccessful attempts—to get to her feet could Ape drag himself away from the sight of this new arrival at Penny Royal. Dawn was breaking as he walked up from the stables to the house.

As he crossed the hall on his way to the kitchen, a hen in the living room announced the laying of an early egg, while in the music room a canary sang its first song of the day. Hearing his footsteps on the great tiled floor of the hall, all the guinea pigs in the dining room began a squealing that said plainly, "Bring us breakfast!" But Ape was too tired to do more than take off his jacket and pull off his boots before dropping onto his bed.

It was past eleven when he woke again and his first thought was that he had fed none of his animals. "Ah, but Jake will have seen to them all!" he said with relief.

Only then did he remember that Jake was now at school.

When at last he had tended to his live-stock (increased yet again, for the gray doe had produced six babies in the butler's pantry), Ape set about getting himself some lunchtime breakfast. Because it was so late, he did not have it in bed but sat at the kitchen table, eating Rice Krispies and squashed-up banana and raspberry yogurt all stirred together.

"How I shall miss that boy when the Harts move on," he said with his mouth full. "I hadn't realized how much he has to do each day. And now there'll be more to do—another litter of little rabbits from the black doe soon, and masses of baby guinea pigs before long. At least the hens can't produce anything, because I haven't got a cockerel, but the canaries probably will. And before you can say Jack Robinson, the puppy will be here. And, of course, there's the baby donkey—I must be sure to give Joe a good price for her when the time comes. Don't know what I'll do without him either. Still, thank goodness Jake *has* gone to school—that should keep them here."

Later that afternoon Ape was standing in the horse stall, feeding an apple to Columbine and telling her how beautiful her daughter was, when Joe and Jake came in.

"I took a few hours off to get some sleep, Mr. Ape," Joe said. "After I'd seen to the horse and donkeys."

"Quite right," said Ape. "What d'you think of the foal, Jake?"

"She's beautiful," said Jake.

"Just what I was telling Columbine. How did you like your first day at the new school?"

"It was all right, Mr. Ape," Jake said, quickly turning away.

"He got into a fight," said his father, "with one of the big boys."

"Really?" said Ape. He took Jake by the shoulders and turned him back around to look at him. "Can't see any cuts or bruises," he said with concern.

"No," said Joe, "but the other boy's got a black eye—a proper shiner."

"He called me names, Mr. Ape," said Jake.

"Like what?"

"He said we were dirty gyppos."

"I bet he won't say that again in a hurry," said Ape.

Quietly, while the boy was talking to the donkey, Joe said to Ape, "I guess it's the best thing that could have happened, really. Jake says they're a nice bunch of kids at that school—except this one who's a bit of a bully. I don't think he'll mess with Jake anymore. The headmaster was very good about it all—pleased, in fact, if you ask me. This other boy has quite a name for throwing his weight about."

"Speaking of names," said Ape, "what are we going to call this foal, Jake?"

Jake smiled.

"I don't really know. I'm so glad I'll be able to watch her grow up."

As long as you and your father don't have to move on, thought Ape, and he suddenly realized with a pang of sadness how lonely he would be if they did.

"Of course, of course," he said gruffly. "Now then, Jake, you choose a name for her. What about a flower? Her mother's named after a flower. Have you got a favorite one?"

Jake thought for a bit, frowning with the effort.

Then he said, "Hollyhock."

"Perfect!" said Ape. "Hollyhock she is. And by the way, she's not the only new arrival. The gray rabbit's had six. Come and have a look."

But when Ape and Jake entered the butler's pantry, they found that the rabbit population of Penny Royal was now two dozen. Within the last few hours the black doe had also given birth to six babies.

"That reminds me. We shall need more rabbit food before long, Mr. Ape," Jake said, "and canary seed."

"Let's go and check up on them," said Ape.

Together they walked across the hall to the first of two smaller rooms that were now used for storage.

The bedding materials, sawdust and straw, and also hay, were kept in the flower room. Here too was kept something Jake had found in the attic, a big old-fashioned baby carriage in which long ago the young Spring-Russells had been wheeled around the grounds of Penny Royal by their nurse-maids. Each day Jake loaded all that he needed into the carriage—food, bedding, sawdust, fresh water in plastic bottles, a broom, a dustpan and brush, a shovel, a bucket—and pushed it around from room to room.

The food supplies were kept in the sewing room, in old cookie tins and tea canisters (also found in the attic). This was the only way to keep the stocks of rabbit mixture and canary seed safe from other greedy little mouths. Ape's pets were not the only creatures in the house—a great many mice lived there as well.

On either side of these small rooms stood two large ones—the library and the billiard room. Ape could not bear to sell the contents of these rooms, and each was unchanged from its original use. Ape loved his books and his billiards, a game he had now begun to teach to Jake (even though the boy was not yet tall enough and had to stand on an apple crate to take his shots).

Now, in the sewing room, Jake checked over the supplies of food as Ape watched.

"I think we'll last till the weekend," he said.

"I can pop down to the pet shop any time," said Ape. "Tomorrow, if you like."

"School," said Jake.

"What? Oh, yes, I get it, you want to come, too. All right, we'll go on Saturday morning."

On Saturday the owner of the pet shop rubbed his hands at the sight of Ape. He knew a good customer when he saw one.

"Good morning, Mr. Spring-Russell!" he said. "What can we do for you today?"

"My assistant has a list of the stuff we need," said Ape. "I'll just have a look round." And leaving Jake in charge, he lumbered off to see what was for sale.

To be fair, Ape had not come with the intention of buying any animals. He took a look at some hamsters (which were all asleep), and at some pet mice ("But we've already got enough of your sort at home," he said).

"Home, sweet home," said a voice. "Bob's your uncle!"

"I beg your pardon?" said Ape, turning to see who had spoken.

But no one was near—Jake and the shopkeeper were busy at the other end of the store, but otherwise it was empty of people.

"Beg your pardon, grant your grace. Mind the cat don't scratch your face," said the voice, and then Ape, looking up, saw in a large cage above his head a green parrot.

"Bob's your uncle!" it said again.

"By Jove!" said Ape. "D'you know, I did have an uncle named Bob! I must say, old chap, you speak extremely well."

"Ding-dong bell," said the parrot. "Pussy's in the well. Pass the mustard. God save the Queen!"

Ape was fascinated by the clarity of the bird's speech.

"I say!" he called to the shopkeeper. "Is this parrot for sale?"

The man came over, Jake following.

"Oh, yes, Mr. Spring-Russell," he said. "He's a wonderful talker, he is. He doesn't make a lot of sense, but he's very quick

at copying things, aren't you, you silly old chap."

"Silly old chap," said the parrot.

"How much d'you want for him?" asked Ape.

"I'm afraid a bird like that is very expensive," said the shopkeeper.

"How much?" asked Ape again, and at the figure the man mentioned, the parrot gave a long low whistle.

"What do you think?" Ape asked the bird.

"Bob's your uncle!" said the parrot.

"Chuck in the cage and a packet of parrot food," said Ape, "and it's a deal."

"A cage like that is very expensive, you know," said the shopkeeper.

"Take it or leave it," Ape said firmly.

"All right, then, Mr. Spring-Russell," said the shopkeeper. "Seeing as you're such a good customer. Mind you, I think you've got a bargain."

"A bargain," said the parrot.

8

Ape Gets Some Advice

ONE EVENING SOME WEEKS later, Joe and Jake sat side by side on the steps of their caravan, enjoying the dusk of an unusually warm October evening. On the grass below them Swift lay on her side, all her pups now gone. Once Ape had taken his pick of the litter, Joe had had no trouble in selling the rest. There were plenty of local sportsmen who knew the potential worth of such lurcher dogs, originally a cross-breed between a greyhound and a collie, so fleet of foot, so quick to pick up the scent of rabbit or even hare on a dark night.

All the pups, a male and three females, had been colored like their mother. Ape had picked the male puppy a week ago.

As they sat and watched the moon

swim up over the rim of the common, Jake said, "I'm worried about Mr. Ape, Dada."

"Worried? Why?"

"Because at the rate he's going, it won't be long before he fills every room in that big house with animals, and then how will he manage when we move on? He's finally released the jackdaw back into the wild, but next time we go to the pet shop, he'll probably come back with mice and gerbils and hamsters, and they'll all start breeding, just like the rabbits and the guinea pigs. There are thirty guinea pigs now, and twenty-four rabbits, and he's put the rabbit does back with the buck, so there'll soon be loads more. Why d'you think he wants so many animals?"

"His wife wouldn't let him keep any," said Joe. "He told me. But you're right, Jake, it's all getting out of hand. And I'll tell you another thing. He's always talking to himself, but now he's forever chatting away to the small animals, to the donkey foal, to the puppy, to the parrot—and of course the parrot talks back. It's getting like a madhouse."

"Mr. Ape's not mad, Dada," said Jake.

"No, I know, he's just a lonely old man. All the same, after what you've said, I'll have a chat with him tomorrow after you've gone to school."

The next day Joe rode Billy the horse up the long drive to Penny Royal, a drive that had once been kept neat and orderly, fringed by well-tended shrubs and bordered iron railings painted white. Now much of the paint had flaked off the rusting rails, the shrubs had grown into a jungle, and the surface of the drive itself was cracked and broken, with weeds sprouting through.

Joe rode across the lawn, which still, despite his best efforts, was not much more than a rough field, to the kitchen garden.

He called to Columbine the donkey, who ambled up, Hollyhock skittering alongside, and he put a halter on her to take her down to water at the stable yard trough. He looked around at the ruins of what had once been the pride of Penny Royal's head gardener, with its orderly plots of vegetables, fine fruit trees that grew against its walls, and its greenhouses; these were now derelict. The donkey had gnawed the bark of the apple, plum, and peach trees, and everywhere was a wild tangle of greenstuff.

Later Joe made his way around to the back door of the house, which led directly into the kitchen. He raised the heavy brass fish-shaped knocker (the Spring-Russell family crest was a leaping salmon) and let it fall.

Before the echoes of the noise had died away, he heard a voice say loudly—in Ape's unmistakable tones—"Kindly go away! I am extremely busy!"

That's not like the old boy, Joe thought. He's usually so polite.

He walked back around the side of the house, only to see Ape coming out the front door carrying his puppy. He marched down the steps and put it on the ground, saying firmly, "Now then, my lad, that's the place to do it—outside. Not in the middle of the hall."

"Sorry about disturbing you just now," said Joe.

"Disturbing me?"

"I knocked on the back door and you said to go away, you were very busy."

Ape gave a roar of laughter. "That must have been Bob," he said. "He's got my voice down to a T."

"The pup looks well," said Joe. "What d'you call him?"

"Speedy," said Ape. "Because he already is. And he's quick to learn, too. That was the first and only mistake we've had in the house—my fault, I should have put him out earlier. Come and have a cup of tea."

In the kitchen the green parrot sat silently in his cage.

"I hear you've been a naughty boy, Uncle Bob," said Ape.

"Kindly go away!" said Uncle Bob. "I am extremely busy!"

"Good imitation, isn't it?" said Ape.

He unlatched the door of the cage, and the parrot emerged slowly, inspecting Joe with a bright considering eye.

"Can he fly?" asked Joe.

"No," said Ape. "He's grounded. His flight feathers on one wing have been clipped."

"Silly old chap," said Uncle Bob in an ordinary parrot voice as he walked up Ape's sleeve and sat on his shoulder.

"He's handsome," said Joe.

"Handsome is as handsome does," said the parrot, and he raised his tail and made a mess on the floor. "Bob's your uncle!" he cried triumphantly.

"I'm afraid his housebreaking isn't going as well as Speedy's," said Ape.

"Good boy, Speedy," said Uncle Bob in

Ape's voice, and the pup's whip tail wagged happily.

After they drank their tea, Ape said, "I haven't collected the eggs today yet. You might like some."

In the living room, while Ape was picking up the eggs, Joe caught the eye of Mrs. Spring-Russell on the wall. What would she say? he thought. What shall *I* say? How shall I start?

Ape's next words gave him the answer to that.

"Only four today," he said, straightening up. "Some of these birds have gone broody, that's the trouble. Now if I only had a cockerel, they could be sitting on fertile eggs, and we could have lots and lots of chicks. Perhaps I should buy one. What do you think, Joe?"

Joe took another look at Mrs. Spring-Russell and a deep breath.

"No, Mr. Ape," he said. "Since you ask me, I certainly don't think you should.

At least in this room the numbers can't increase, or in the music room where the canaries are all male birds. Because before long you're going to have a plague of rabbits and guinea pigs in the dining room, and then you'll be starting to fill the upstairs rooms, and where will it all end? It's not really my business, but I think you should be getting rid of animals, not getting more."

"Get rid of them all?" said Ape. "Not Speedy?"

"No, of course not."

"Or Hollyhock?"

"No, of course not."

"Or Uncle Bob?"

"No, of course not!" shouted the parrot.

"What I mean is," said Joe, "why not sell the babies you've bred? All those little rabbits, and then all the little guinea pigs. There are thirty of those already, Jake said."

"Thirty-five," said Ape. "Another litter last night."

"There you are, you see. Think of all the children who'd love to have one or two of those as pets."

"But I don't know any children," said Ape. "Except Jake."

"I do," said Joe. "All the kids at his school. They'd take them."

"I suppose you're right," said Ape. "But even if I did that, there'd soon be lots more babies."

"If you keep both sexes. Why not just keep the doe rabbits and the guinea-pig sows? And don't buy a cockerel."

"And Bob's your uncle," said the parrot.

9

Ape Starts a Fire

FOR THE REST OF THE week Ape considered Joe's advice. That weekend he consulted Jake. They were playing a game of billiards at the time, and Jake, standing on his apple crate, was lining up a shot for a pocket at the far end of the table.

"Jake!" said Ape suddenly just as the boy began to shoot.

"Mr. Ape!" said Jake. "You threw me off!"

"Sorry," said Ape. "I was just going to ask you to do me a favor."

"What sort of a favor?"

"Well, you see..." began Ape, and he outlined his plan.

"If I write it all out," he said, "could you take the note to your headmaster and see if it's okay by him?"

Jake nodded.

"Thanks," said Ape. "Look, take that shot again."

But once more, just as the boy's cue approached the ball, Ape's voice rang out, saying, "Jake!"

This time Jake missed the ball completely. "Oh, honestly, Mr. Ape...!" he began, but when he turned around, Ape was shaking his head and grinning and pointing to a chair with Uncle Bob perched on the back.

"Foul stroke," said the parrot.

Ape gave a lot of thought to the wording of the note that Jake was to take to school on Monday. He wanted to be sure that any animal he parted with would be properly looked after, and though he didn't intend to ask any money for his creatures, he thought that getting something for nothing was not a good idea.

So the note that Jake took (and that the headmaster approved) read as follows:

Rabbits—guinea pigs—canaries. If you would like one or more of any of these animals, all you have to do is write a letter to Mr. Spring-Russell of Penny Royal. The letter must state what you want and explain why you want it and how you will look after it.

Letters must be accompanied by a note from your parents giving their permission.

The writers of the best letters will each receive the animals of their choice as a prize—free.

"There!" Ape had said as he finished writing this at the kitchen table. "What d'you think of that, then, boys?" And Jake had said, "Fine," and Speedy had thumped his tail on the floor, and Uncle Bob had said, "Kindly go away! I am extremely busy!"

By the end of October, Ape's menagerie

had grown very, very much smaller. Many children had written wanting rabbits or guinea pigs or canaries, and Ape hadn't had the heart to refuse any of them. (A surprising number of applicants claimed that Jake Hart was their best friend.) Not only had the buck rabbit and all the babies gone but two of the does as well, leaving only the spotted doe. She and two female guinea pigs (all the rest had been snapped up) had now been moved from the dining room to share the music room with its last remaining inhabitant, a male canary who sang happily to them from his golf-club swing.

Speedy and Uncle Bob still lived in the kitchen, of course, and the hens in the living room, but the animal population of Penny Royal had dwindled to almost nothing.

Ape found that he could not regret this, for he had made a great many children happy. Joe was glad that no more animals of any kind could be born in the house. Jake was not sorry to have less to do—it gave him more time for his homework—and he was pleased because the parrot seemed to have taken a great liking to him. Whenever Jake was in the house, Uncle Bob would follow him around with his bowlegged walk, shouting, "Jake! Jake! Wait for me! Bob's your uncle!"

One morning at the beginning of November, Ape said to Joe, "I'm just on my way into town. It's Guy Fawkes Night this coming Sunday, and I thought I'd buy a nice bunch of fireworks. Haven't had any for years and years, but I always enjoyed them as a boy. Jake would enjoy it, wouldn't he?"

"He would," said Joe. "So would I."

As usual, the anniversary of English conspirator Guy Fawkes's failed attempt to blow up King James I and all the members of Parliament on November 5, 1605, would be celebrated throughout Great Britain.

So Ape went off and had a wonderful

time buying rockets and Roman candles and sparklers.

As it grew dark on Sunday evening, everything was ready. Safety was, as always on Guy Fawkes Night, the main thing to be thought of, not just for people but for animals, too. Swift had been left at home in the caravan. Speedy was shut in the kitchen with Uncle Bob. The horse and donkeys were far enough away so as to be in no danger, and the hens and the remaining small animals were perfectly safe inside the house.

Ape and Joe had made a big pile of old scraps of wood and other trash in the middle of the sweep of gravel in front of the front door. In the center was a scarecrow meant to represent Guy Fawkes, dressed in some of Ape's old clothes (and looking not unlike him).

Once it was dark enough, they set it alight.

Jake stood watching the bonfire,

twirling a sparkler, as the poor old "Guy Fawkes" burned and fell. Then the two men began to set off the fireworks, and the rockets soared and the Roman candles flared. And all the time the bonfire blazed and the sparks shot upward into the night sky.

So busy were they all with the fireworks that no one noticed when some old, very dry planks of wood in the middle of the bonfire suddenly collapsed, sending up a pillar of fat sparks.

No one saw the wind catch one of those sparks and lift it high onto the roof of Penny Royal.

No one knew that just at that point of the roof stood the tall chimney stack of the disused living room fireplace. Nor did they know that in the top of that chimney were the remains of the rescued jackdaw's nest, a collection of pieces of paper, straw, and old sticks.

For hundreds of years jackdaws had nested in the tops of this and the many other chimneys of Penny Royal. But now they never would do so in this chimney again.

The single spark fell into this old nest and set the paper and straw on fire, and then the sticks caught alight and began to burn fiercely. Unknown to all those below, this fireball fell down the dining room chimney onto the hearth beneath, where, as they blazed up, the flames took hold of the varnished wood on the great mahogany mantelpiece above the fireplace. The terrified hens, awakened suddenly from their murmuring slumber, fluttered from their perches, and began to run blindly around the huge high-ceilinged room.

10

Ape Hits Rock Bottom

NOT UNTIL THE FINAL rocket was lit—an especially big one that Ape had saved for the end—did anyone notice anything.

As he had done with all the other rockets, Ape aimed it well away from the house. But this last one decided to swerve violently in flight and burst right above Penny Royal, sending out a great shower of golden globes.

As the watchers looked at these floating gently earthward and vanishing one by one, Joe suddenly noticed smoke coming out of one of the chimney stacks.

"Look, Mr. Ape!" he called, pointing upward.

"Blimey O'Reilly!" cried Ape. "That's the living room chimney! Something's on fire!"

"I'll go and have a look through the French windows. Jake, you stay here away from the fire," ordered Joe, and he ran around the side of the house, carrying the pitchfork with which he had been stoking the bonfire.

Ape made for the front door.

By the time Joe reached the French windows of the living room, the room was well alight, and through the glass Joe saw the frantic hens fluttering up and down in the glare of the flames.

Joe tried the handles of the windows, but they were locked on the inside. Quickly, with several strong blows of the pitchfork, he smashed the windows, and the twelve hens scuttled wildly out and stumbled away over the ruined lawns into the darkness.

Fanned now by the wind that blew in through the shattered windows, the flames leaped higher within the living room, until the inner door caught fire. From the wall

the blazing portrait of Mrs. Spring-Russell in her blue ball gown fell crashing to the floor.

Ape, crossing the hall, saw the burning living room door and heard the crackle of the flames. His immediate thoughts were to save his animals and his house, in that order. The creatures in the music room were most at risk, he knew, because if the fire got into the hall, they might be cut off.

Hurriedly he opened a closet where coats and hats and canes were kept, and also, he knew, an old suitcase.

In the music room he caught the spotted doe rabbit and the two guinea pigs and thrust them into the suitcase. Then he managed to grab the canary from its golf-club swing.

Holding the bird in one large hand and the suitcase in the other, he went back into the hall, only to find that the fire had burst out of the living room and that now a wall of flames barred his way to the kitchen. And in the kitchen was where Speedy and Uncle Bob were!

Somehow Ape made his way back to the front door, his only way out now, and stumbled down the steps.

So relieved was he to see two figures approaching, Jake with Speedy on a leash and Joe carrying the parrot in his cage, that it took him a moment to remember that, although the animals were rescued, he'd done nothing yet to save the house.

"The fire department!" he said. "We must telephone the fire department!"

"Jake's done it, Mr. Ape," said Joe. "He dialed Emergency while I was getting the animals out, even though I told him to stay out of the house."

"Good boy!" said Ape.

"We got out of the kitchen just in time," said Joe. "It'll be completely in flames by now. As the whole house will be before long, I'm afraid."

Which, by the time the fire department arrived, it was.

The firefighters did their best, running hoses up from the stable yard and aiming them at the inferno, but they were fighting a losing battle.

Penny Royal, given to Ape's ancestor by Charles II, burned to the ground on the very day that, nearly 400 years earlier, Guy Fawkes had tried to kill King Charles's grandfather, James I.

Meanwhile, by the light of the flames Joe and Jake managed to find all the dazed hens that were squatting in the shrubs and flower beds and put them in the kitchen garden, where Columbine and Hollyhock were. There they would at least be safe for the night—no fox could climb those walls. In there, too, were put the rabbit and the guinea pigs.

As for the canary, Joe offered to take it back to the caravan. "I've still got my father's old canary cage," he said.

"All right," said Ape wearily.

"Now, Mr. Ape," said Joe. "You must get some rest. Where will you sleep tonight?"

"Sleep?" said Ape. "I don't know." He shook his head. "I don't know," he said again.

"Mr. Ape," said Jake, "you could sleep in the Rolls-Royce. On the backseat. It'd be very comfy. There's that big car rug to keep you warm."

Ape managed a smile.

"Jake," he said, "I don't know what I'd do without you."

"Good boy, Jake," said Uncle Bob.

Much later, long after Joe and Jake had gone, the fire captain came to Ape.

"I'm sorry, Mr. Spring-Russell," he said. "There wasn't much we could do. The fire had taken too strong a hold by the time we got here. Any idea what started it?"

Ape looked down sadly.

"We had a bonfire," he said, "and some fireworks."

The firefighter nodded. "November the fifth," he said with a sigh. "Not one of our favorite nights, I'm afraid. Your family lived here long, sir?"

"More than three hundred years," said Ape.

"You on your own now?"

"Yes."

"Look on the bright side, sir," said the firefighter. "Think what you can do with the insurance money. You could build yourself a nice little bungalow here with all the modern conveniences. Ah, well, there's nothing more we can do tonight. We've damped it all down. We'll be back in the morning to have a look round, but to tell the truth, there's not much left to burn."

Even after the fire department had coiled their hoses and left, Ape still stood before the ruins of the house, his dog at his side, his parrot on his shoulder.

Once the fire had consumed the ground floor, it had raged upward to the second and third floors and the attic. And the fifteen bedrooms and all the other rooms of the upper part of the house had fallen into the burned-out remains of the living room and dining room, of the music room and sewing room, of the flower room and library and billiard room and butler's pantry, and, of course, on the gutted kitchen and the glowing ashes of Ape's four-poster bed.

All that remained were the outer walls, whose stones the fire could not destroy.

At last, Ape turned and shambled away, his long arms hanging low, while behind him, in the coming light of dawn, wisps of smoke still curled from the gaping blackened window holes of the great house called Penny Royal.

11

Ape Buys a House

WHEN APE WOKE UP next morning, for a moment he could not think where on earth he was. He was looking up at a roof not far above his head, the roof, it seemed, of a car.

Then he realized that he was lying, his knees drawn right up, across the backseat of the old Rolls-Royce, the Silver Ghost, in the coach house of the stable block.

Throwing off the car rug that covered him, Ape struggled to sit up and stretch out his cramped legs. From the front he heard the slap of a tail on the seat cushions, and then Speedy's narrow head appeared over the top of the passenger seat. Uncle Bob perched on top of the steering wheel.

Sometimes by sheer luck the parrot said the correct thing, as now, when he wished Ape a good morning.

"Good morning, Uncle Bob," replied Ape, but to himself he said that it was a terrible morning. His home, which had been the home of his family for so long, was no more. The great house was gone.

Wearily, the old man put his head in his hands.

Joe saw him sitting like this when he entered the coach house, Swift at his heels. Poor old fellow, he thought. What's to become of him? Quietly he went out again, picked up an empty bucket, and let it fall on the cobbles with a loud clang.

In a few moments Ape appeared, yawning and stretching.

"Good morning, Mr. Ape," said Joe. "You could do with some breakfast, I expect?"

"Not hungry," said Ape.

"Look," said Joe. "Why not drive into

town and go to a café and have a good breakfast? Leave Speedy here with Swift if you like, and the parrot, too, if you think he'll stay with me."

"I am extremely busy," said Uncle Bob.

"I'll put him in the kitchen garden till you get back, Mr. Ape," said Joe. "He can't get out of there, and he can have a nice chat with the hens."

"Silly old chap," said the parrot.

As Ape drove the Rolls out of the coach house, something felt wrong to him. He glanced at himself in the rear-view mirror and saw what it was. He had no hat. His old brown bowler had, of course, been burned to gray ashes in the hall closet along with all the other hats and coats and canes.

Then it occurred to him that all his clothes were gone. He owned none except what he now wore—his hairy tweed suit, one shirt, his old school tie, and his brown boots.

"One thing's certain," he said as he

drove up to the common. "I must buy myself some sort of cot. I can't sleep another night in this car—I'm as stiff as a board. Oh, dear, what's to become of me?"

But half an hour later, he felt much better. He'd found that he was, in fact, starving hungry, and he'd had a splendid breakfast—eggs, bacon, sausages, mushrooms, and fried bread.

Leaving the café, Ape bought a local newspaper and sat in the Rolls to read it. His eye was immediately caught by an item in red print at the bottom of the front page.

SPECIAL EDITION
STATELY HOME BURNED TO GROUND

Last night was, literally, Bonfire Night for Penny Royal, home of Mr. A. P. E. Spring-Russell. This magnificent house, which has belonged to the Spring-Russell family for more than three centuries, was reduced to a shell by an all-consuming blaze that the local fire department was powerless to control. Neither Mr. Spring-Russell nor a family of

Gypsies at present camping on the common, who were the only witnesses, were able to say exactly what caused the fire.

Ape gave a deep sigh. Then he said, "No use crying over spilt milk," and opened the paper.

By chance he opened it to the classifieds, at a column titled CARAVANS.

Ape stared at the word unseeingly, his mind still filled with yesterday's drama, his bones aching from his less-than-comfortable night's sleep in the car.

"Much as I love you, old girl," he said to the Silver Ghost, "you are not the most relaxing place to sleep," and then he focused properly on that word *caravans,* and suddenly he knew exactly what he was going to do.

"Golly whiskers!" he cried. "I'll buy one! I'll buy myself a caravan! Today. Now. This very minute." And he began to read the column carefully.

The biggest local suppliers of house trailers, mobile homes, and the like, it seemed, was Comfihome Caravans, so he started the car and drove off.

Ape parked the Rolls in front of the caravan center and went in.

A number of different types of caravans were parked in rows, and a smooth-looking young salesman came forward.

Funny-looking old customer, this one, he thought as Ape shambled toward him, long arms hanging. He noted the suit, the shirt, the tie, all crumpled and dirty from the smoke and filth of the fire, and the brown boots badly in need of polish. Tramp, is he? the salesman said to himself. Looks as though he's slept in his clothes. Which, of course, Ape had.

Managing to stop himself from saying, "What do you want?" the salesman said instead, "Can I help you?" It did not occur to him to say sir.

"Yes," said Ape. "You can sell me a caravan. I shall want it delivered today. I've no tow bar on the old girl." And he pointed to the Silver Ghost and produced a gold credit card from his pocket.

"Yes, sir, yes, sir, certainly, sir," said the salesman. "What type had you in mind?"

"Smallest possible," said Ape. "It's just for me."

"Even our smallest one accommodates two, sir," said the salesman.

"Well, actually, we're three altogether," said Ape. "Me and my puppy and my parrot. Just show me the smallest one you've got. All I need is a bed, a table, and something to cook on."

"Oh, it will have all those and much more," said the salesman. "Including a chemical toilet."

"A what?" said Ape. "Oh, yes, I see what you mean."

So that afternoon a Land Rover from Comfihome Caravans towed into the stable yard at Penny Royal a Bijou Roadmaster de Luxe, and that night Ape and Speedy settled down happily in it, Ape in a comfortable sofa bed just long enough for him, Speedy on a rug on the floor, while, from the parrot cage hanging above, Uncle Bob's final sleepy words were "Home, sweet home."

12

Ape Makes a Decision

IT MUST HAVE BEEN that little item in the local newspaper that did it:

"A family of Gypsies at present camping on the common...the only witnesses..."

Tongues began to wag.

The fire at Penny Royal was a topic of much interest in the town, and the probable cause of it was plain—in the minds of certain spiteful people. Wherever two or three were gathered together, the same comments could be heard:

"What was a family of Gypsies doing up there anyway?"

"You can't trust 'em. Sly bunch, they are."

"Dirty diddikais."

"Shouldn't be surprised if they started the fire."

"Cooking hedgehogs, I daresay. They do, you know."

"Sooner they're off the common, the better."

It wasn't long before some people had convinced themselves, and others, that it was indeed the Gypsies who had, for dark reasons of their own, deliberately burned down Penny Royal.

Soon Joe became aware that the locals were looking at him differently. Before, they had simply disregarded him, giving him a nod at best and never speaking to him, but now there was staring and pointing and the passing of remarks.

Waiting to collect his son from school, Joe overheard two mothers talking:

"Weather's got a lot colder," said one in a loud voice.

"Yes," said the other. "You need a nice fire in the house."

"Not too big a fire," said the first. "You don't want to burn the house down."

"No," said the second. "Not like some people."

Jake had made quite a few friends, but some of the other schoolchildren now began to treat him differently. Nobody actually called him a dirty gyppo, because they remembered what had happened to the bully boy. But there was whispering and giggling and talk behind his back. Jake was made to feel unlike the other children, whose clothes were nicer, who had expensive toys to play with and real houses to live in, and all this began to make him unhappy.

But Ape, unaware of these problems, was happy in his caravan, as he was when training his dog Speedy or taking his donkey Hollyhock for a walk or feeding his rabbit or his guinea pigs, which now lived in a horse's stall. The hens were a bit of a disappointment now, for the shock of the fire had completely stopped them from laying, and Ape was again having to buy his eggs.

But all the time the grim ruins of the house stood in the background, constantly catching his eye and casting a shadow over his other pleasures.

By now Ape had had the Rolls fitted with a tow bar, and was having fun pulling the new caravan up and down the drive and practicing reversing. One day when he had towed the caravan down to the end of the drive with Speedy and Uncle Bob aboard it, the thought of escape suddenly occurred to him.

"Suppose I just kept on driving," he said. "Driving anywhere, any direction, any distance, towing my nice new home behind me. I'd never have to look at those terrible, accusing, fire-blackened walls again. I couldn't do it today, of course. There's too much to fix up first—there's the land to be sold, and the stable block— just right for conversion it would be, make a nice house for someone, though not for me. But what fun it would be to make a completely fresh start, a new life in some other part of the country, and then to be free to move on again whenever I felt like it, as the Gypsies do."

Even as he spoke these last words, he realized that this plan was only pie in the sky. "But then if I did that, I'd lose my friends Joe and Jake."

He turned and drove back to the stable block.

• ▲ •

One evening in early December, Ape was at the propane gas stove in his caravan, cooking his supper (canned mushroom soup with cocktail sausages and baked beans in it), when there was a knock at the door.

"Kindly go away!" said Uncle Bob in Ape's voice. "I am extremely busy!"

"Who is it?" said Ape.

"It's me, Mr. Ape—Joe."

"Come in, Joe, come in!" called Ape. "Sit down, do. What's the matter? Nothing wrong with any of the animals, is there?"

"No," said Joe. "But there is something wrong."

"What?" said Ape.

"Persecution, I suppose you could call it," said Joe, and he told Ape all about the rumors that had circulated after the fire, and about the dislike—hatred, even—of him and his son that this talk had inspired among many of the local people.

"Folks cross the road to avoid meeting me now," he said, "and Jake's unhappy at school. It's the old story, Mr. Ape, that all Romany people know. Every man's hand is against the Gypsies. Except yours. You have always been good to us."

"This is terrible, Joe!" exclaimed Ape. "That people should spread such lies. Why, you and Jake risked your lives to save the puppy and the parrot. If anyone burned the house down, I did. I should never have built that bonfire so close."

Speedy whined softly at the sadness in his master's voice, and Uncle Bob, sitting as usual on Ape's shoulder, gently nibbled at the lobe of his ear.

"I've come to tell you that I've made up my mind, Mr. Ape," said Joe. "Again, I'm sorry, truly sorry, but again, it's for the good of my boy."

"Made up your mind to do what?" said Ape.

"To leave. To move on once more, away from here. To take to the open road."

Ape thrust out a hand and Joe took it.

"I wish with all my heart," Joe said, "that we did not have to part."

"We don't," said Ape. "I'm coming, too."

⬭ 13 ⬭

Ape Hits the Trail

HIS MIND MADE UP, Ape could hardly wait to go. But of course there was much to be done first.

On one thing Ape was determined. If Joe and Jake were leaving soon, he wasn't going to hang around Penny Royal by himself to settle up all his affairs. His house might be gone, but his money wasn't. He was still a rich man, and when the fire-insurance claim was paid and the land and the stable block sold, he would be that much richer.

So he called upon the services of a lot of other people to do the work for him—his bank manager, his accountant, his investment adviser, his insurance agent, and the best of the local real-estate agents.

"You fix everything up for me," he told them, "and then get in touch with me when it's all settled."

"But where will you be?" each asked.

"No idea," said Ape, "but I'll keep you posted."

The other question that needed settling was the animals' welfare. What was to be done about them?

Ape and Joe discussed this.

"You'd better keep the canary," Ape said. "He's happy with you, and he'll be more comfortable riding along with you nice and slowly. He'd swing about all over the place once I speed up in the Rolls."

Joe smiled, thinking that Ape's usual stately rate of progress would be even slower when towing the heavy caravan. "Very well, Mr. Ape," he said. "We'll take the bird, and of course we'll have Billy pulling the caravan, and Columbine and Hollyhock will be tethered behind us."

"Well, you've got things all figured

out," said Ape. "As for me, I shall take my dog, of course, as you will, and my parrot, but I don't know quite what to do with the spotted rabbit and the two guinea pigs. Jake could have them for a Christmas present if you've got room for them."

Joe thought for a moment, and then he said, "Pannier baskets."

"I don't follow you," said Ape.

"We've got a pair of panniers—big wicker baskets with lids we sling over Columbine's back, one on either side. They could travel in those."

"Great!" said Ape. "That only leaves the hens. I don't think the old girls are suited to life in a caravan."

"Well," said Joe, "they're still only laying one or two eggs a day between the twelve of them. I would sell them. Someone will get some nice Sunday dinners out of them."

In fact, Ape gave the hens away to the mailman, who kept chickens. He did not tell Joe that he had extracted a promise from the man that they would not be eaten.

Ape and the Harts had decided between them that they would not set out before the end of Jake's term at school. Because this was not until December 22, they then decided to wait until after Christmas.

Ape bought maps, and he and Joe pored over them.

"We must have a good start on you, Mr. Ape," Joe said, "because you'll go ten times as fast as we shall. If you follow the same route, then once you catch up with us, we can look about for a suitable place to stay. Which direction do you fancy taking? It's all the same to us."

"West, I think," said Ape. "We'll go west out of Gloucestershire and across the river Severn and into the Welsh hills."

So they settled on a route as free from traffic as possible, along lanes and byways, and on an eventual meeting place. Joe and Jake would set out on Boxing Day, the

British holiday on the day after Christmas. Ape, because it would give them six days' start and because he thought it a suitable date to begin a new life, would leave on New Year's Day.

On Christmas Day, Ape gave another party—a caravan-warming party he called it.

Joe had driven his own caravan down from the common and up the drive, to park it next to Ape's caravan in the stable yard, ready for departure the next morning.

Then they all three squeezed into the Bijou Roadmaster de Luxe, and ate a huge tea, including a Christmas cake that Ape had specially ordered. On top of it were two caravans, one drawn by a 50-horse-power car, one by a single horse.

When they had finished their tea, Ape opened a bottle of wine, and he and Joe raised their glasses (and Jake raised his soda), and they drank a toast.

"Good luck!" said Ape, and "Good luck!" replied Joe and Jake and Uncle Bob.

Jake looked worried at parting from his friend the next morning.

"You *will* come, Mr. Ape, won't you?" he said anxiously. "You will follow us?"

"I will, Jake," said Ape. "Cross my heart."

· ▄ ·

At the top of the drive he stood the following morning, Speedy beside him, Uncle Bob on his shoulder, watching and waving as the caravan, drawn by Billy, the two donkeys walking behind, grew smaller and smaller until it vanished from his sight.

"Right," said Ape. "Let's have some breakfast. What d'you say to that, Uncle Bob?"

"Great!" said the parrot in Ape's voice.

"Kippers and custard," said Ape. "That's what I fancy." This meant, in Ape's language, smoked herring with scrambled eggs.

After that, he ate his favorite mess of creamed rice and strawberry jam and crumbled-up graham crackers.

Later, when he'd fed his animals, Ape decided to go for a walk. He asked Uncle Bob if he would like to come, but the parrot told him he was extremely busy, so Ape set off with his dog.

Jake had tried his best to teach Ape to whistle the way he did, but Ape was hopeless at it. Still, he'd come to a sort of agreement with Speedy. He would put two fingers into his mouth and make a sort of puffing noise, which was all he could manage, and Speedy (if he was near enough to hear) would come to him.

Ape walked up the long drive and then onto the common, where the Gypsy caravan had stood. Looking back from this viewpoint, he could see the whole estate of Penny Royal laid out below.

At that distance it was not possible to distinguish the chaos of the kitchen garden or the wreck of the lawns or the jungle of the shrubs. Even the ruins of the house looked, at this range, romantic.

Ape stood on the common for a long time, looking down, and as he did so he suddenly realized that he no longer felt guilty about what had happened. Try as he would, he could not make himself believe that generations of past Spring-Russells were turning in their graves at the thought that their descendant was about to desert the family house.

"It's dead and gone," he said to Speedy, "like them, and in six days' time we'll be going, you and I and Uncle Bob. Then you'll see your mum again and I'll see my friends. Come on, let's go home now, back to our nice new caravan. Because that's what it is from now on—our home, no matter where we are. It ought to have a name, really, I suppose."

Those six days seemed to drag by, so eager was Ape to be gone and on the trail of Joe and Jake, but at last it was the final day of the old year. Only then did it suddenly become clear to Ape that there was only one thing to call his new home, now that his old one was gone in all but name. So he made a last trip to the hardware store and bought a small can of paint and a brush.

Had there been any people around very early on the morning of New Year's Day, they would have seen an old Rolls-Royce Silver Ghost pull away from the stable block and set off slowly down the drive, towing a large new caravan in which, had they known it, were a dog and a green parrot. A caravan on whose door was newly painted in small neat lettering:

PENNY ROYAL

At the wheel of the Rolls they would have seen a large, long-armed old man wearing a hairy tweed suit and his old school tie and brown boots. Above all, perhaps, they would have noted what a huge, happy, excited grin there was on the face of Archibald Peregrine Edmund Spring-Russell, the man called Ape.

ABOUT THE AUTHOR

DICK KING-SMITH was born and raised in Gloucestershire, England. He served in the Grenadier Guards during World War II, then returned home to Gloucestershire to realize his lifelong ambition of farming. After twenty years as a farmer, he turned to teaching and then to writing the children's books that have earned him many fans on both sides of the Atlantic. Inspiration for his writing has come from his farm and his animals.

Among his well-loved novels are *Babe: The Gallant Pig, Harry's Mad, Martin's Mice, Ace: The Very Important Pig, Three Terrible Trins, Harriet's Hare, The Stray*, and *A Mouse Called Wolf*. In 1992 he was named Children's Author of the Year at the British Book Awards. In 1995 *Babe: The Gallant Pig* became a critically acclaimed major motion picture.